THE EMPIRE OF
THE NECROMANCERS
AND THREE OTHERS

THE EMPIRE OF
THE NECROMANCERS
AND THREE OTHER TALES

CLARK ASHTON SMITH

WILDSIDE PRESS

THE EMPIRE OF THE NECROMANCERS
AND THREE OTHERS

Copyright © 2009 by Wildside Press LLC.
www.wildsidebooks.com

"The Empire of Necromancers" originally appeared in *Weird Tales*, September 1934. "The Enchantress of Sylaire" originally appeared in *Weird Tales*, July 1941. "The Invisible City" originally appeared in *Wonder Stories*, June 1932. "Mother of Toads" originally appeared in *Weird Tales*, July 1938.

CONTENTS

The Empire of the Necromancers 7

The Enchantress of Sylaire 16

The Invisible City 31

Mother of Toads 51

THE EMPIRE OF
THE NECROMANCERS

THE LEGEND of Mmatmuor and Sodosma shall arise only in the latter cycles of Earth, when the glad legends of the prime have been forgotten. Before the time of its telling, many epochs shall have passed away, and the seas shall have fallen in their beds, and new continents shall have come to birth. Perhaps, in that day, it will serve to beguile for a little the black weariness of a dying race, grown hopeless of all but oblivion. I tell the tale as men shall tell it in Zothique, the last continent, beneath a dim sun and sad heavens where the stars come out in terrible brightness before eventide.

I

MMATMUOR AND SODOSMA were necromancers who came from the dark isle of Naat, to practise their baleful arts in Tinarath, beyond the shrunken seas. But they did not prosper in Tinarath, for death was deemed a holy thing by the people of that gray country; and the nothingness of the tomb was not lightly to be desecrated; and the raising up of the dead by necromancy was held in abomination.

So, after a short interval, Mmatmuor and Sodosma were driven forth by the anger of the inhabitants and were compelled to flee toward Cincor, a desert of the south, which was peopled only by the bones and mummies of a race that the pestilence had slain in former time.

The land into which they went lay drear and leprous and ashen below the huge, ember-colored sun. Its crumbling rocks and deathly solitudes of sand would have struck terror to the hearts of common men; and, since they had been thrust out in that barren place without food or sustenance, the plight of the sorcerers might well have seemed a desperate one. But, smiling secretly, with the air of conquerors who tread the approaches of a long-coveted realm, Sodosma and Mmatmuor walked steadily on into Cincor

Unbroken before them, through fields devoid of trees and grass, and across the channels of dried-up rivers, there ran the great highway by which travelers had gone formerly between Cincor and Tinarath. Here they met no living thing, but soon they came to the skeletons of a horse and its rider lying full in the road and wearing still the sumptuous harness and raiment which they had worn in the flesh. And Mmatmuor aad Sodosma paused before the piteous bones, on which no shred of corruption remained, and they smiled evilly at each other.

"The steed shall be yours," said Mmatmuor, "since you are a little the elder of us two and are thus entitled to precedence, and the rider shall serve us both and be the first to acknowledge fealty to us in Cincor."

Then, in the ashy sand by the wayside, they drew a threefold circle and, standing together at its center, they performed the abominable rites that compel the dead to arise from tranquil nothingness and obey henceforward, in all things, the dark will of the necromancer. Afterward, they sprinkled a pinch of magic powder on the nostril-holes of the man and the horse, and the white bones, creaking mournfully, rose up from where they had lain, and stood in readiness to serve their masters.

So, as had been agreed between them, Sodosma mounted the skeleton steed and took up the jeweled reins, and rode in an evil mockery of Death on his pale horse; while Mmatmuor trudged on beside him, leaning lightly on an ebon staff; and the skeleton of the man, with its rich raiment flapping loosely, followed behind the two like a servitor.

After a while, in the gray waste, they found the remnant of another horse and rider, which the jackals had spared and the sun had dried to the leanness of old mummies. These also they raised up from death, and Mmatmuor bestrode the withered charger, and the two magicians rode on in state like errant emperors, with a lich and a skeleton to attend them. Other bones and charnel remnants of men and beasts to which they came anon were duly resurrected in like fashion so that they gathered to themselves an everswelling train in their progress through Cincor.

Along the way, as they neared Yethlyreom, which had been the capital, they found numerous tombs and necropoli, inviolate still after many ages and containing swathed mummies that had scarcely withered in death. All these they raised up and called from sepulchral night to do their bidding. Some they commanded to sow and till the desert fields and hoist water from the sunken wells; others they left at diverse tasks, such as the mummies had performed in life. The century-long silence was broken by the noise and tumult of myriad activities, and the lank liches of weavers toiled at their shuttles, and the corpses of plowmen followed their furrows behind carrion oxen.

Weary with their strange journey and their oft-repeated incantations, Mmatmuor and Sodosma saw before them at last, from a desert hill, the lofty spires and fair, unbroken domes of Yethlyreom, steeped in the darkening stagnant blood of ominous sunset.

"It is a goodly land," said Mmatmuor, "and you and I will share it between us, and hold dominion over all its dead, and be crowned as emperors on the morrow in Yethlyreom."

"Aye," replied Sodosma, "for there is none living to dispute us here, and those that we have summoned from the tomb shall move and breathe only at our dictation and may not rebel against us."

So, in the blood-red twilight that thickened with purple, they entered Yethlyreom and rode on among the lofty, lampless mansions and installed themselves with their grisly retinue in that stately and abandoned palace where the dynasty of Nimboth emperors had reigned for two thousand years with dominion over Cincor.

In the dusty golden halls, they lit the empty lamps of onyx by means of their cunning sorcery and supped on royal viands, provided from past years, which they evoked in like manner. Ancient and imperial wines were poured for them in moonstone cups by the fleshless hands of their servitors, and they drank and feasted and revelled in fantasmagoric pomp, deferring till the morrow the resurrectiom of those who lay dead in Yethlyreom.

They rose betimes, in the dark crimson dawn, from the opulent palace-beds in which they had slept, for much remained to be done. Everywhere in that forgotten city, they went busily to and fro, working their spells on the people that had died in the last year of the pest and had lain unburied. And having accomplished this, they passed beyond Yethlyreom into that other city of high tombs and mighty mausoleums, in which lay the Nimboth emperors and the more consequential citizens and nobles of Cincor.

Here, they bade their skeleton slaves to break in the sealed doors with hammers; and then, with their sinful, tyrannous incantations, they called forth the imperial mummies, even to the eldest of the dynasty, all of whom came walking stiffly, with lightless eyes, in rich swathings sewn with flame-bright jewels. And also, later, they brought forth to a semblance of life many generations of courtiers and dignitaries.

Moving in solemn pageant, with dark and haughty and hollow faces, the dead emperors and empresses of Cincor made obeisance to Mmatmuor and Sodosma and attended them like a train of captives through all the streets of Yethlyreom. Afterward, in the immense throne-room of the palace, the necromancers mounted the high double throne, where the rightful rulers had sat with their consorts. Amid the assembled emperors, in gorgeous and funereal state, they were invested with sovereignty by the sere hands of the mummy of Hestaiyon, earliest of the Nimboth line, who had ruled in half-mythic years. Then all the descendants of Hestaiyon, crowding the room in a great throng, acclaimed with toneless, echo-like voices the dominion of Mmatmuor and Sodosma.

Thus did the outcast necromancers find for themselves an empire and a subject people in the desolate, barren land where the men of Tinarath had driven them forth to perish. Reigning supreme over all the dead of Cincor, by virtue of their malign magic, they exercised a baleful despotism. Tribute was borne to them by fleshless porters from outlying realms, and plague-eaten corpses and tall mummies scented with mortuary balsams went to and fro upon their errands in Yethlyreom, or heaped before their greedy eyes, from inexhaustible vaults, the cobweb-blackened gold and dusty gems of antique time.

Dead laborers made their palace-gardens to bloom with long-perished flowers; liches and skeletons toiled for them in the mines, or reared superb, fantastic towers to the dying sun. Chamberlains and princes of old time were their cupbearers, and stringed instruments were plucked for their delight by the slim hands of empresses with golden hair that had come forth untarnished from the night of the tomb. Those that were fairest, whom the plague and the worm had not ravaged overmuch, they took for their lemans and made to serve their necrophilic lust.

II

IN ALL things, the people of Cincor performed the actions of life at the will of Mmatmuor and Sodosma. They spoke, they moved, they ate and drank as in life. They heard and saw and felt with a similitude of the senses that had been theirs before death; but their brains were enthralled by a dreadful necromancy. They recalled but dimly their former existence, and the state to which they had been summoned was empty and troublous and shadowlike. Their blood ran chill and sluggish, mingled with water of Lethe; and the vapors of Lethe clouded their eyes.

Dumbly they obeyed the dictates of their tyrannous lords, without rebellion or protest, but filled with a vague, illimitable weariness such as the dead must know when, having drunk of eternal sleep, they are called back once more to the bitterness of mortal being. They knew no passion or desire or delight, only the black languor of their awakening from Lethe, and a gray, ceaseless longing to return to that interrupted slumber.

Youngest and last of the Nimboth emperors was Illeiro, who had died in the first month of the plague and had lain in his high-built mausoleum for two hundred years before the coming of the necromancers.

Raised up with his people and his fathers to attend the tyrants, Illeiro had resumed the emptiness of existence without question and had felt no surprise. He had accepted his own resurrection and that of his ancestors as one accepts the indignities and marvels of a dream. He knew that he had come back to a faded sun, to a hollow and spectral world, to an order of things in which his place was merely that of an obedient shadow. But at first he was troubled only, like the others, by a dim weariness and pale hunger for the lost oblivion.

Drugged by the magic of his overlords, weak from the age-long nullity of death, he beheld like a somnambulist the enormities to which his fathers were subjected. Yet, somehow, after many days, a feeble spark awoke in the sodden twilight of his mind.

Like something lost and irretrievable, beyond prodigious gulfs, he recalled the pomp of his reign in Yethlyreom, and the golden pride and exultation that had been his in youth. And, recalling it, he felt a vague stirring of revolt, a ghostly resentment against the magicians who had haled him forth to this calamitous mockery of life. Darkly he began to grieve for his fallen state and the mournful plight of his ancestors and his people.

Day by day, as a cup-bearer in the halls where he had ruled aforetime, Illeiro saw the doings of Mmatmuor and Sodosma. He saw their caprices of cruelty and lust, their growing drunkenness and gluttony. He watched them wallow in their necromantic luxury and become lax with indolence, gross with indulgence, They neglected the study of their art; they forgot many of their spells. But still they ruled, mighty and formidable; and, lolling on couches of purple and rose, they planned to lead an army of the dead against Tinarath.

Dreaming of conquest and of vaster necromancies, they grew fat and slothful as worms that have installed themselves in a charnel rich with corruption. And pace by pace with their laxness and tyranny, the fire of rebellion mounted in the shadowy heart of Illeiro like a flame that struggles with Lethean damps. And slowly, with the waxing of his wrath, there returned to him something of the strength and firmness that had been his in life. Seeing the turpitude of the oppressors and knowing the wrong that had been done to the helpless dead, he heard in his brain the clamor of stifled voices demanding vengeance.

Among his fathers, through the palace-halls of Yethlyreom, Illeiro moved silently at the bidding of the masters, or stood awaiting their command. He poured in their cups of onyx the amber vintages, brought by wizardry from hills beneath a younger sun; he submitted to their contumelies and insults. And, night by night, he watched them nod in their drunkenness till they fell asleep, flushed and gross amid their arrogated splendor.

There was little speech among the living dead, and son and father, daughter and mother, lover and beloved, went to and fro without sign of recognition, making no comment on their evil lot. But at last, one midnight, when the tyrants lay in slumber and the flames wavered in the necromantic lamps, Illeiro took counsel with Hestaiyon, his eldest ancestor, who had been famed as a great wizard in fable and was reputed to have known the secret lore of antiquity.

Hestaiyon stood apart from the others, in a corner of the shadowy hall. He was brown and withered in his crumbling mummy-cloths, and his lightless obsidian eyes appeared to gaze still upon nothingness. He seemed not to have heard the questions of Illeiro; but at length, in a dry, rustling whisper, he responded:

"I am old, and the night of the sepulcher was long, and I have forgotten much. Yet, groping backward across the void of death, it may be that I shall retrieve something of my former wisdom, and between us we shall devise a mode of deliverance." And Hestaiyon searched among the shreds of memory as one who reaches into a place where the worm has been and the hidden archives of old time have rotted in their covers till at last he remembered and said:

"I recall that I was once a mighty wizard, and among other things, I knew the spells of necromancy, but employed them not, deeming their use and the raising up of the dead an abhorrent act. Also, I possessed other knowledge, and perhaps among the remnants of that ancient lore, there is something which may serve to guide us now. For I recall a dim, dubitable prophecy, made in the primal years at the founding of Yethlyreom and the empire of Cincor. The prophecy was that an evil greater than death would befall the emperors and the people of Cincor in future times, and that the first and the last of the Nimboth dynasty, conferring together, would effect a mode of release and the lifting of the doom. The evil was not named in the prophecy, but it was said that the two emperors would learn the solution of their problem by the breaking of an ancient clay image that guards the nethermost vault below the imperial palace in Yethlyreom."

Then, having heard this prophecy from the faded lips of his forefather, Illeiro mused a while and said:

"I remember now an afternoon in early youth, when searching idly through the unused vaults of our palace as a boy might do, I came to the last vault and found therein a dusty, uncouth image of clay whose form and countenance were strange to me. And, knowing not the prophecy, I turned away in disappointment and went back as idly as I had come to seek the moted sunlight."

Then, stealing away from their heedless kinfolk, and carrying jeweled lamps they had taken from the hall, Hestaiyon and Illeiro went downward by subterranean stairs beneath the palace and, threading like implacable furtive shadows the maze of nighted corridors, they came at last to the lowest crypt.

Here, in the black dust and clotted cobwebs of an immemorial past, they found, as had been decreed, the clay image whose rude features were those of a forgotten earthly god. And Illeiro shattered the image with a fragment of stone, and he and Hestaiyon took from its hollow center a great sword of unrusted steel, and a heavy key of untarnished bronze, and tablets of bright brass on which were inscribed the various things to be done so that Cincor should be rid of the dark reign of the necromancers and the people should win back to oblivious death.

So, with the key of untarnished bronze, Illeiro unlocked, as the tablets had instructed him to do, a low and narrow door at the end of the nethermost vault, beyond the broken image; and he and Hestaiyon saw, as had been prophesied, the coiling steps of somber stone that led downward to an undiscovered abyss where the sunken fires of earth still burned. And leaving Illeiro to ward the open door, Hestaiyon took up the sword of unrusted steel in his thin hand and went back to the hall where the necromancers slept, lying a-sprawl on their couches of rose and purple, with the wan, bloodless dead about them in patient ranks.

Upheld by the ancient prophecy and the lore of the bright tablets, Hestaiyon lifted the great sword and struck off the head of Mmatmuor and the head of Sodosma, each with a single blow. Then, as had been directed, he quartered the remains with mighty strokes. And the necromancers gave up their unclean lives and lay supine, without movement, adding a deeper red to the rose and a brighter hue to the sad purple of their couches.

Then, to his kin who stood silent and listless, hardly knowing their liberation, the venerable mummy of Hestaiyon spoke in sere murmurs, but authoritatively, as a king who issues commands to his children. The dead emperors and empresses stirred like autumn leaves in a sudden wind, and a whisper passed among them and went forth from the palace, to be communicated at length, by devious ways, to all the dead of Cincor.

All that night and during the blood-dark day that followed, by wavering torches or the light of the failing sun, an endless army of plague-eaten liches, of tattered skeletons, poured in a ghastly torrent through the streets of Yethlyreom and along the palace-hall where Hestaiyon stood guard above the slain necromancers. Unpausing, with vague, fixed eyes, they went on like driven shadows to seek the subterraaean vaults below the palace, to pass through the open door where Illeiro waited in the last vault, and then to wend downward by a thousand thousand steps to the verge of that gulf in which boiled the ebbing fires of Earth. There, from the verge, they flung themselves to a second death and the clean annihilation of the bottomless flames.

But, after all had gone to their release, Hestaiyon still remained, alone in the fading sunset, beside the cloven corpses of Mmatmuor and Sodosma. There, as the tablets had directed him to do, he made trial of those spells of elder necromancy which he had known in his former wisdom, and cursed the dismembered bodies with that perpetual life-in-death which Mmatmuor and Sodosma had sought to inflict upon the people of Cincor. And maledictions came from the pale lips, and the heads rolled horribly with glaring eyes, and the limbs and torsos writhed on their imperial couches amid clotted blood. Then, with no backward look, knowing that all was done as had been ordained and predicted from the first, the mummy of Hestaiyon left the necromancers to their doom and went wearily through the nighted labyrinth of vaults to rejoin Illeiro.

So, in tranquil silence, with no further need of words, Illeiro and Hestaiyon passed through the open door of the nether vault, and Illeiro locked the door behind them with its key of untarnished bronze. And thence, by the coiling stairs, they wended their way to the verge of the sunken flames and were one with their kinfolk and their people in the last, ultimate nothingness.

But of Mmatmuor and Sodosma, men say that their quartered bodies crawl to and fro to this day in Yethlyreom, finding no peace or respite from their doom of life-in-death and seeking vainly through the black maze of nether vaults the door that was locked by Illeiro.

THE ENCHANTRESS
OF SYLAIRE

"WHY, you big ninny! I could never marry you," declared the demoiselle Dorothée, only daughter of the Sieur des Flèches. Her lips pouted at Anselme like two ripe berries. Her voice was honey — but honey filled with bee-stings. "You are not so ill-looking. And your manners are fair. But I wish I had a mirror that could show you to yourself for the fool that you really are."

"Why?" queried Anselme, hurt and puzzled.

"Because you are just an addle-headed dreamer, pouring over books like a monk. You care for nothing but silly old romances and legends. People say that you even write verses. It is lucky that you are at least the second son of the Comte du Framboisier — for you will never be anything more than that."

"But you loved me a little yesterday," said Anselme bitterly. A woman finds nothing good in the man she has ceased to love.

"Dolt! Donkey!" cried Dorothée, tossing her blond ringlets in pettish arrogance. "If you were not all that I have said, you would never remind me of yesterday. Go, idiot — and do not return."

ANSELME, the hermit, had slept little, tossing distractedly on his hard, narrow pallet. His blood, it seemed, had been fevered by the sultriness of the summer night.

Then, too, the natural heat of youth had contributed to his unease. He had not wanted to think of women — a certain woman in particular. But, after thirteen months of solitude in the heart of the wild woodland of Averoigne, he was still far from forgetting. Crueller even than her taunts was the remembered beauty of Dorothée des Flèches: the full-ripened mouth, the round arms and slender waist, the breast and hips that had not yet acquired their amplest curves.

Dreams had thronged the few short intervals of slumber, bringing other visitors, fair but nameless, about his couch.

He rose at sundown, weary but restless. Perhaps he would find refreshment by bathing, as he had often done, in a pool fed from the river Isoile and hidden among alder and willow thickets. The water, deliciously cool at that hour, would assuage his feverishness.

His eyes burned and smarted in the morning's gold glare when he emerged from the hut of wattled osier withes. His thoughts wandered, still full of the night's disorder. Had he been wise, after all, to quit the world, to leave his friends and family and seclude himself because of a girl's unkindness? He could not deceive himself into thinking that he had become a hermit through any aspiration toward sainthood, such as had sustained the old anchorites. By dwelling so much alone, was he not merely aggravating the malady he had sought to cure?

Perhaps, it occurred to him belatedly, he was proving himself the ineffectual dreamer, the idle fool that Dorothée had accused him of being. It was weakness to let himself be soured by a disappointment.

Walking with downcast eyes, he came unaware to the thickets that fringed the pool. He parted the young willows without lifting his gaze and was about to cast off his garments. But at that instant the nearby sound of splashing water startled him from his abstraction.

With some dismay, Anselme realized that the pool was already occupied. To his further consternation, the occupant was a woman. Standing near to the center, where the pool deepened, she stirred the water with her hands till it rose and rippled against the base of her bosom. Her pale wet skin glistened like white rose-petals dipped in dew.

Anselme's dismay turned to curiosity and then to unwilling delight. He told himself that he wanted to withdraw but feared to frighten the bather by a sudden movement. Stooping with her clear profile and her shapely left shoulder toward him, she had not perceived his presence.

A woman, young and beautiful, was the last sight he had wished to see. Nevertheless, he could not turn his eyes away. The woman was a stranger to him, and he felt that she was no girl of the village or countryside. She was lovely as any chatelaine of the great castles of Averoigne. And yet surely no lady or demoiselle would bathe unattended in a forest pool.

Thick-curling chestnut hair, bound by a light silver fillet, billowed over her shoulders and burned to red, living gold where the sun-rays searched it out through the foliage. Hung about her neck, a light, golden chain seemed to reflect the lusters of her hair, dancing between her breasts as she played with the ripples.

The hermit stood watching her like a man caught in webs of sudden sorcery. His youth mounted within him in response to her beauty's evocation.

Seeming to tire of her play, she turned her back and began to move toward the opposite shore where, as Anselme now noticed, a pile of feminine garments lay in charming disorder on the grass. Step by step she rose from the shoaling water, revealing hips and thighs like those of an antique Venus.

Then, beyond her, he saw that a huge wolf, appearing furtively as a shadow from the thicket, had stationed itself beside the heap of clothing. Aoselme had never seen such a wolf before. He remembered the tales of werewolves that were believed to infest that ancient wood, and his alarm was touched instantly with the fear which only preternatural things can arouse. The beast was strangely colored, its fur being a glossy bluish-black. It was far larger than the common gray wolves of the forest. Crouching inscrutably, half hidden in the sedges, it seemed to await the woman as she waded shoreward. Another moment, thought Anselme, and she would perceive her danger, would scream and turn in terror. But still she went on, her head bent forward as if in serene meditation.

"Beware the wolf!" he shouted, his voice strangely loud and seeming to break a magic stillness. Even as the words left his lips, the wolf trotted away and disappeared behind the thickets toward the great elder forest of oaks and beeches. The woman smiled over her shoulder at Anselme, turning a short oval face with slightly slanted eyes and lips red as pomegranate flowers. Apparently she was neither frightened by the wolf nor embarrassed by Anselme's presence.

"There is nothing to fear," she said in a voice like the pouring of warm honey. "One wolf, or two, will hardly attack me."

"But perhaps there are others lurking about," persisted Anselme. "And there are worse dangers than wolves for one who wanders alone and unattended through the forest of Averoigne. When you have dressed, with your permission, I shall attend you safely to your home, whether it be near or far."

"My home lies near enough in one sense, and far enough in another," returned the lady cryptically. "But you may accompany me there, if you wish."

She turned to the pile of garments, and Anselme went a few

paces away among the alders and busied himself by cutting a stout cudgel for weapon against wild beasts or other adversaries. A strange but delightful agitation possessed him, and he nearly nicked his fingers several times with the knife. The misogyny that had driven him to a woodland hermitage began to appear slightly immature, even juvenile. He had let himself be wounded too deeply and too long by the injustice of a pert child.

By the time Anselme finished cutting his cudgel, the lady had completed her toilet. She came to meet him, swaying like a lamia. A bodice of vernal green velvet, baring the upper slopes of her breasts, clung tightly about her as a lover's embrace. A purple velvet gown, flowered with pale azure and crimson, moulded itself to the sinuous outlines of her hips and legs. Her slender feet were enclosed in fine soft leather buskins, scarlet-dyed, with tips curling pertly upward. The fashion of her garments, though oddly antique, confirmed Anselme in his belief that she was a person of no common rank.

Her raiment revealed, rather than concealed, the attributes of her femininity. Her manner yielded — but it also withheld.

Anselme bowed before her with a courtly grace that belied his rough country garb.

"Ah! I can see that you have not always been a hermit," she said, with soft mockery in her voice.

"You know me, then," said Anselme.

"I know many things. I am Sephora, the enchantress. It is unlikely that you have heard of me, for I dwell apart, in a place that none can find — unless I permit them to find it."

"I know little of enchantment," admitted Anselme. "But I can believe that you are an enchantress."

For some minutes they had followed a little used path that serpented through the antique wood. It was a path the hermit had never come upon before in all his wanderings. Lithe saplings and low-grown boughs of huge beeches pressed closely upon it. Anselme, holding them aside for his companion, came often in thrilling contact with her shoulder and arm. Often she swayed against him, as if losing her balance on the rough ground. Her weight was a delightful burden, too soon relinquished. His pulses coursed tumultuously and would not quiet themselves again.

Anselme had quite forgotten his eremitic resolves. His blood and his curiosity were excited more and more. He ventured various gallantries, to which Sephora gave provocative replies. His questions, however, she answered with elusive vagueness. He could learn nothing, could decide nothing, about her. Even her age puzzled him. At one moment, he thought her a young girl; the next, a mature woman.

Several times, as they went on, he caught glimpses of black fur beneath the low, shadow foliage. He felt sure that the strange black wolf he had seen by the pool was accompanying them with a furtive surveillance. But, somehow, his sense of alarm was dulled by the enchantment that had fallen upon him.

Now the path steepened, climbing a densely wooded hill. The trees thinned to straggly, stunted pines, encircling a brown, open moorland as the tonsure encircles a monk's crown. The moor was studded with Druidic monoliths dating from ages prior to the Roman occupation of Averoigne. Almost at its center, there towered a massive cromlech consisting of two upright slabs that supported a third like the lintel of a door. The path ran straight to the cromlech.

"This is the portal of my domain," said Sephora, as they neared it. "I grow faint with fatigue. You must take me in your arms and carry me through the ancient doorway."

Anselme obeyed very willingly. Her cheeks paled, her eyelids fluttered and fell as he lifted her. For a moment, he thought that she had fainted, but her arms crept warm and clinging around his neck.

Dizzy with the sudden vehemence of his emotion, he carried her through the cromlech. As he went, his lips wandered across her eyelids and passed deliriously to the soft red flame of her lips and the rose pallor of her throat. Once more she seemed to faint beneath his fervor.

His limbs melted and a fiery blindness filled his eyes. The earth seemed to yield beneath them like an elastic couch as he and Sephora sank down.

Lifting his head, Anselme looked about him with swiftly growing bewilderment. He had carried Sephora only a few paces — and yet the grass on which they lay was not the sparse and sun-dried grass of the moor, but was deep, verdant, and filled with tiny vernal blossoms! Oaks and beeches, huger even than those of the familiar forest, loomed umbrageously on every hand with masses of new, golden-green leafage, where he had thought to see the open upland. Looking back, he saw that the gray, lichened slabs of the cromlech itself alone remained of that former landscape.

Even the sun had changed its position. It had hung at Anselme's left, still fairly low in the east, when he and Sephora had reached the moorland. But now, shining with amber rays through a rift in the forest, it had almost touched the horizon on his right.

He recalled that Sephora had told him she was an enchantress. Here, indeed, was proof of sorcery! He eyed her with curious doubts and misgivings,

"Be not alarmed," said Sephora, with a honeyed smile of reassurance. "I told you that the cromlech was the doorway to my domain. We are now in a land lying outside of time and space as you have hitherto known them. The very seasons are different here. But there is no sorcery involved, except that of the great ancient Druids, who knew the secret of this hidden realm and reared those mighty slabs for a portal between the worlds. If you should weary of me, you can pass back at any time through the doorway. But I hope that you have not tired of me so soon —"

Anselme, though still bewildered, was relieved by this information. He proceeded to prove that the hope expressed by Sephora was well-founded. Indeed, he proved it so lengthily and in such detail that the sun had fallen below the horizon before Sephora could draw a full breath and speak again.

"The air grows chill," she said, pressing against him and shivering lightly. "But my home is close at hand."

They came in the twilight to a high, round tower among trees and grass-grown mounds.

"Ages ago," announced Sephora, "there was a great castle here. Now the tower alone remains, and I am its chatelaine, the last of my family. The tower and the lands about it are named Sylaire."

Tall, dim tapers lit the interior, which was hung with rich arrases, vaguely and strangely pictured. Aged, corpse-pale servants in antique garb went to and fro with the furtiveness of specters, setting wines and foods before the enchantress and her guest in a broad hall. The wines were of rare flavor and immense age, the foods were curiously spiced. Anselme ate and drank copiously. It was like some fantastic dream, and he accepted his surroundings as a dreamer does, untroubled by their strangeness.

The wines were potent, drugging his senses into warm oblivion. Even stronger was the inebriation of Sephora's nearness. However, Anselme was a little startled when the huge black wolf he had seen that morning entered the hall and fawned like a dog at the feet of his hostess.

"You see, he is quite tame," she said, tossing the wolf bits of meat from her plate. "Often I let him come and go in the tower, and sometimes he attends me when I go forth from Sylaire."

"He is a fierce-looking beast," Anselme observed doubtfully. It seemed that the wolf understood the words, for he bared his teeth at Anselme with a hoarse, preternaturally deep growl. Spots of red fire glowed in his somber eyes like coals fanned by devils in dark pits.

"Go away, Malachie," commanded the enchantress sharply. The wolf obeyed her, slinking from the hall with a malign backward glance at Anselme.

"He does not like you," said Sephora. "That, however, is perhaps not surprising."

Anselme, bemused with wine and love, forgot to inquire the meaning of her last words.

MORNING came too soon, with upward-slanting beams that fired the tree-tops around the tower.

"You must leave me for awhile," said Sephora, after they had breakfasted. "I have neglected my magic of late — and there are matters into which I should inquire."

Bending prettily, she kissed the palms of his hands. Then, with backward glances and smiles, she retired to a room at the tower's top beside her bed-chamber. Here, she had told Anselme, her grimoires and potions and other appurtenances of magic were kept.

During her absence, Anselme decided to go out and explore the woodland about the tower. Mindful of the black wolf, whose tameness he did not trust despite Sephora's reassurances, he took with him the cudgel he had cut that previous day in the thickets.

There were paths everywhere, all leading to fresh loveliness. Truly, Sylaire was a region of enchantment. Drawn by the dreamy golden light and the breeze laden with the freshness of spring flowers, Anselme wandered on from glade to glade.

He came to a grassy hollow where a tiny spring bubbled from beneath mossed boulders. He seated himself on one of the boulders, musing on the strange happiness that had entered his life so unexpectedly. It was like one of the old romances, the tales of glamor and fantasy, that he had loved to read. Smiling, he remembered the gibes with which Dorothée des Flèches had expressed her disapproval of his taste for such reading-matter. What, he wondered, would Dorothée think now? At any rate, she would hardly care —

His reflections were interrupted. There was a rustling of leaves, and the black wolf emerged from the boscage in front of him, whining as if to attract his attention. The beast had somehow lost his appearance of fierceness.

Curious and a little alarmed, Anselme watched in wonder while the wolf began to uproot with his paws certain plants that somewhat resembled wild garlic. These he devoured with palpable eagerness.

Anselme's mouth gaped at the thing which ensued. One moment the wolf was before him. Then, where the wolf had been, there rose up the figure of a man, lean, powerful, with blue-black hair and beard, and darkly flaming eyes. The hair grew almost to his brows, the beard nearly to his lower eye-lashes. His arms, legs, shoulders, and chest were matted with bristles.

"Be assured that I mean you no harm," said the man. "I am Malachie du Marais, a sorcerer and the one-time lover of Sephora. Tiring of me and fearing my wizardry, she turned me into a werewolf by giving me secretly the waters of a certain pool that lies amid this enchanted domain of Sylaire. The pool is cursed from old time with the infection of lycanthropy — and Sephora has added her spells to its power. I can throw off the wolf shape for a little while during the dark of the moon. At other times, I can regain my human form, though only for a few minutes, by eating the root that you saw me dig and devour, The root is very scarce."

Anselme felt that the sorceries of Sylaire were more complicated than he had hitherto imagined. But amid his bewilderment, he was unable to trust the weird being before him. He had heard many tales of werewolves, who were reputedly common in medieval France. Their ferocity, people said, was that of demons rather than of mere brutes.

"Allow me to warn you of the grave danger in which you stand," continued Malachie du Marais. "You were rash to let yourself be enticed by Sephora. If you are wise, you will leave the purlieus of Sylaire with all possible dispatch. The land is old in evil and sorcery, and all who dwell within it are ancient as the land and are equally accursed. The servants of Sephora, who waited upon you yestereve, are vampires that sleep by day in the tower vaults and come forth by night. They go out through the Druid portal to prey on the people of

Averoigne."

He paused as if to emphasize the words that followed. His eyes glittered balefully, and his deep voice assumed a hissing undertone. "Sephora herself is an ancient lamia, well-nigh immortal, who feeds on the vital forces of young men. She has had many lovers throughout the ages — and I must deplore, even though I cannot specify, their ultimate fate. The youth and beauty that she retains are illusions. If you could see Sephora as she really is, you would recoil in revulsion, cured of your perilous love. You would see her unthinkably old and hideous with infamies."

"But how can such things be?" queried Anselme. "Truly, I cannot believe you."

Malachie shrugged his hairy shoulders. "At least I have warned you. But the wolf-change approaches, and I must go. If you will come to me later, in my abode which lies a mile to the westward of Sephora's tower, perhaps I can convince you that my statements are the truth. In the meanwhile, ask yourself if you have seen any mirrors, such as a beautiful young woman would use, in Sephora's chamber. Vampires and lamias are afraid of mirrors — for a good reason."

ANSELME went back to the tower with a troubled mind. What Malachie had told him was incredible. Yet there was the matter of Sephora's servants. He had hardly noticed their absence that morning — and yet he had not seen them since the previous eve. And he could not remember any mirrors among Sephora's various feminine belongings.

He found Sephora awaiting him in the tower's lower hall. One glance at the utter sweetness of her womanhood, and he felt ashamed of the doubts which Maiachie had inspired in him.

Sephora's blue-gray eyes questioned him, deep and tender as those of some pagan goddess of love. Reserving no detail, he told her of his meeting with the werewolf.

"Ah! I did well to trust my intuitions," she said. "Last night, when the black wolf growled and glowered at you, it occurred to me that he was perhaps becoming more dangerous than I had realized. This morning, in my chamber of magic, I made use of my clairvoyant powers, and I learned much. Indeed, I have been careless. Malachie has become a menace to my security. Also, he hates you, and would destroy our happiness."

"Is it true, then," questioned Anselme, "that he was your lover, and that you turned him into a werewolf?"

"He was my lover — long, long ago. But the werewolf form was his own choice, assumed out of evil curiosity by drinking from the pool of which he told you. He has regretted it since, for the wolf shape, while giving him certain powers, in reality limits his actions and his sorceries. He wishes to return to human shape and, if he succeeds, will become doubly dangerous to us both.

"I should have watched him well — for I now find that he has stolen from me the recipe of antidote to the werewolf waters. My clairvoyance tells me that he has already brewed the antidote, in the brief intervals of humanity regained by chewing a certain root. When he drinks the potion, as I think that he means to do before long, he will regain human form permanently. He waits only for the dark of the moon, when the werewolf spell is at its weakest."

"But why should Malachie hate me?" asked Anselme. "And how can I help you against him?"

"That first question is slightly stupid, my dear. Of course, he is jealous of you. As for helping me — well, I thought of a good trick to play on Malachie."

She produced a small purple glass vial, triangular in shape, from the folds of her bodice.

"This vial," she told him, "is filled with the water of the werewolf pool. Through my clairvoyant vision, I learned that Malachie keeps his newly brewed potion in a vial of similar size, shape and color. If you can go to his den and substitute one vial for the other without detection, I believe that the results will be quite amusing."

"Indeed, I will go," Anselme assured her.

"The present should be a favorable time," said Sephora. "It is now within an hour of noon, and Malachie often hunts at this time. If you should find him in his den, or he should return while you are there, you can say that you came in response to his invitation."

She gave Anselme careful instructions that would enable to find the werewolf's den without delay. Also, she gave him a sword, saying that the blade had been tempered by the chanting of magic spells that made it effective against such beings as Malachie.

"The wolf's temper has grown uncertain," she warned. "If he should attack you, your alder stick would prove a poor weapon..."

*   *   *

IT WAS easy to locate the den, for well-used paths ran toward it with little deviation. The place was the mounded remnant of a tower that had crumbled down into grassy earth and mossy blocks. The entrance had once been a lofty doorway; now it was only a hole, such as a large animal would make in leaving and returning to its burrow.

Anselme hesitated before the hole.

"Are you there, Malachie du Marais?" he shouted.

There was no answer, no sound of movement from within. Anselme shouted once more. At last, stooping on hands and knees, he entered the den.

Light poured through several apertures, latticed with wandering tree-roots, where the mound had fallen in from above. The place was a cavern rather than a room. It stank with carrion remnants into whose nature Anselme did not inquire too closely. The ground was littered with bones, broken stems and leaves of plants, and shattered or rusted vessels of alchemic use. A verdigris-eaten kettle hung from a tripod above ashes and ends of charred faggots. Rain-sodden grimoires lay mouldering in rusty metal covers. The three legged ruin of a table was propped against the wall. It was covered with a medley of oddments, among which Anselme discerned a purple vial resembling the one given him by Sephora.

In one corner was a litter of dead grass. The strong, rank odor of a wild beast mingled with the carrion stench.

Anselme looked about and listened cautiously. Then, without delay, he substituted Sephora's vial for the one on Malachie's table. The stolen vial he placed under his jerkin.

There was a padding of feet at the cavern's entrance. Anselme turned — to confront the black wolf. The beast came toward him, crouching tensely as if about to spring, with eyes glaring like crimson coals of Avernus. Anselme's fingers dropped to the hilt of the enchanted sword that Sephora had given him.

The wolf's eyes followed his fingers. It seemed that he recognized the sword. He turned from Anselme and began to chew some roots of the garlic-like plant, which he had doubtless collected to make possible those operations which he could hardly have carried on in wolfish form.

This time, the transformation was not complete. The head, and body of Malachie du Marais rose up again before Anselme; but the legs were the hind legs of a monstrous wolf. He was like some bestial hybrid of antique legend.

"Your visit honors me," he said, half snarling, with suspicion in his eyes, and voice. "Few have cared to enter my poor abode, and I am grateful to you. In recognition of your kindness, I shall make you a present."

With the padding movements of a wolf, he went over to the ruinous table and groped amid the confused oddments with which it was covered. He drew out an oblong silver mirror, brightly burnished, with a jeweled handle such as a great lady or damsel might own. This he offered to Anselme.

"I give you the mirror of Reality," he announced. "In it, all things are reflected according to their true nature. The illusions of enchantment cannot deceive it. You disbelieved me, when I warned you against Sephora. But if you hold this mirror to her face and observe the reflection, you will see that her beauty, like everything else in Sylaire, is a hollow lie — the mask of ancient horror and corruption. If you doubt me, hold the mirror to my face — now: for I, too, am part of the land's immemorial evil."

Anselme took the silver oblong and obeyed Malachie's injunction. A moment, and his nerveless fingers almost dropped the mirror. He had seen reflected within it a face that the sepulcher should have hidden long ago.

The horror of that sight had shaken him so deeply that he could not afterwards recall the circumstances of his departure from the werewolf's lair. He had kept the werewolf's gift, but more than once he had been prompted to throw it away. He tried to tell himself that what he had seen was merely the result of some wizard trick. He refused to believe that any mirror would reveal Sephora as anything but the young and lovely sweetheart whose kisses were still warm on his lips.

All such matters, however, were driven from Anselme's mind by the situation that he found when he re-entered the tower hall. Three visitors had arrived during his absence. They stood fronting Sephoia, who, with a tranquil smile on her lips, was apparently trying to explain something to them. Anselme recognized the visitors with much amzement, not untouched with consternation.

One of them was Dorothée des Flèches, clad in a trim traveling habit. The others were two serving men of her father, armed with longbows, quivers of arrows, broadswords, and daggers. In spite of this array of weapons, they did not look any too comfortable or at home. But Dorothée seemed to have retained her usual matter-of-fact assurance.

"What are you doing in this queer place, Anselme?" she cried. "And who is this woman, this chatelaine of Sylaire, as she calls herself?"

Anselme felt that she would hardly understand any answer that he could give to either query. He looked at Sephora, then back at Dorothée. Sephora was the essence of all the beauty and romance that he had ever craved. How could he have fancied himself in love with Dorothée, how could he have spent thirteen months in a hermitage because of her coldness and changeability? She was pretty enough, with the common bodily charms of youth. But she was stupid, wanting in imagination — prosy already in the flush of her girlhood as a middle-aged housewife. Small wonder that she had failed to understand him.

"What brings you here?" he countered. "I had not thought to see you again."

"I missed you, Anselme," she sighed. "People said that you had left the world because of your love for me and had become a hermit. At last I came to seek you. But you had disappeared. Some hunters had seen you pass yesterday with a strange woman, across the moor of Druid stones. They said you had both vanished beyond the cromlech, fading as if in air. Today I followed you with my father's serving men. We found ourselves in this strange region, of which no one has ever heard. And now this woman —"

The sentence was interrupted by a mad howling that filled the room with eldritch echoes. The black wolf, with jaws foaming and slavering, broke in through the door that had been opened to admit Sephora's visitors. Dorothée des Fleches began to scream as he dashed straight toward her, seeming to single her out for the first victim of his rabid fury.

Something, it was plain, had maddened him. Perhaps the water of the werewolf pool, substituted for the antidote, had served to redouble the original curse of lycanthropy.

The two serving men, bristling with their arsenal of weapons, stood like effigies. Anselme drew the sword given him by the enchantress and leaped forward between Dorothée and the wolf. He raised his weapon, which was straight-bladed and suitable for stabbing. The mad werewolf sprang as if hurled from a catapult, and his red, open gorge was spitted on the out-thrust point. Anselme's hand was jarred on the sword-hilt, and the shock drove him backward. The wolf fell thrashing at Anselme's feet. His jaws had clenched on the blade. The point protruded beyond the stiff bristles of his neck.

Anselme tugged vainly at the sword. Then the black-furred body ceased to thrash — and the blade came easily. It had been withdrawn from the sagging mouth of the dead ancient sorcerer, Malachie du Marais, which lay before Anselme on the flagstones. The sorcerer's face was now the face that Anselme had seen in the mirror, when he held it up at Malachie's injunction.

"You have saved me! How wonderful!" cried Dorothée.

Anselme saw that she had started toward him with out-thrust arms. A moment more, and the situation would become embarrassing.

He recalled the mirror, which he had kept under his jerkin, together with the vial stolen from Malachie du Marais. What, he wondered, would Dorothée see in its burnished depths?

He drew the mirror forth swiftly and held it to her face as she advanced upon him. What she beheld in the mirror he never knew, but the effect was startling. Dorothée gasped, and her eyes dilated in manifest horror. Then, covering her eyes with her hands, as if to shut out some ghastly vision, she ran shrieking from the hall. The serving men followed her. The celerity of their movements made it plain that they were not sorry to leave this dubious lair of wizards and witches.

Sephora began to laugh softy. Anselme found himself chuckling. For a while, they abandoned themselves to uproarious mirth. Then Sephora sobered.

"I know why Malachie gave you the mirror," she said. "Do you not wish to see my reflection in it?"

Anselme realized that he still held the mirror in his hand. Without answering Sephora, he went over to the nearest window, which looked down on a deep pit lined with bushes, that had been part of an ancient, half-filled moat. He hurled the silver oblong into the pit.

"I am content with what my eyes tell me, without the aid of any mirror," he declared. "Now let us pass to other matters which have been interrupted too long."

Again the clinging deliciousness of Sephora was in his arms, and her fruit-soft mouth was crushed beneath his hungry lips.

The strongest of all enchantments held them in its golden circle.

THE INVISIBLE CITY

"CONFOUND YOU," said Langley in a hoarse whisper that came with effort through swollen lips, blue-black with thirst. "You've gulped about twice your share of the last water in the Lob-nor Desert." He shook the canteen which Furnham had just returned to him and listened with a savage frown to the ominously light gurgling of its contents.

The two surviving members of the Furnham Archaeological Expedition eyed each other with newborn but rapidly growing disfavor. Furnham, the leader, flushed with dark anger beneath his coat of deepening dust and sunburn. The accusation was unjust, for he had merely moistened his parched tongue from Langley's canteen. His own canteen, which he had shared equally with his companion, was now empty.

Up to that moment, the two men had been the best of friends. Their months of association in a hopeless search for the ruins of the semi-fabulous city of Kobar had given them abundant reason to respect each other. Their quarrel sprang from nothing else than the mental distortion and morbidity of sheer exhaustion, and the strain of a desperate predicament. Langley, at times, was even growing a trifle light-headed after their long ordeal of wandering on foot through a land without wells, beneath a sun whose flames poured down upon them like molten lead.

"We ought to reach the Tarim River pretty soon," said Furnham stiffly, ignoring the charge and repressing a desire to announce in mordant terms his unfavorable opinion of Langley.

"If we don't, I guess it will be your fault," the other snapped. "There's been a jinx on this expedition from the beginning, and I shouldn't wonder if the jinx were you. It was your idea to hunt for Kobar, anyway. I've never believed there was any such place."

Furnham glowered at his companion, too near the breaking point himself to make due allowance for Langley's nerve-wrought condition, and then turned away, refusing to reply. The two plodded on, ignoring each other with sullen ostentatiousness.

The expedition, consisting of five Americans in the employ of a New York museum, had started from Khotan two months before to investigate the archaeological remains of Eastern Turkestan. Ill-luck had dogged them continually, and the ruins of

Kobar — their main objective, said to have been built by the ancient Uighurs — had eluded them like a mirage. They found other ruins, had exhumed a few Greek and Byzantine coins and a few broken Buddhas, but nothing of much novelty or importance, from a museum viewpoint.

At the very outset, soon after leaving the oasis of Tchertchen, one member of the party had died from gangrene caused by the vicious bite of a Bactrian camel. Later on, a second, seized by a cramp while swimming in the shallow Tarim Kver, near the reedy marshes of Lob-nor, that strange remnant of a vast inland sea, had drowned before his companions could reach him. A third had died of some mysterious fever. Then in the desert south of the Tarim, where Furnham and Langley still persisted in a futile effort to locate the lost city, their Mongol guides had deserted them. They took all the camels and most of the provisions, leaving to the two men only their rifles, their canteens, their other personal belongings, the various antique relics they had amassed, and a few tins of food.

The desertion was hard to explain, for the Mongols had heretofore shown themselves reliable enough. However, they had displayed a queer reluctance on the previous day, had seemed unwilling to venture further among the endless undulations of coiling sand and pebbly soil.

Furnham, who knew the language better than Langley, had gathered that they were afraid of something, were deterred by superstitious legends concerning this portion of the Lob-nor Desert. But they had been strangely vague and reticent as to the object of their fear, and Furnham had learned nothing of its actual nature.

Leaving everything but their food, water, and rifles to the mercy of the drifting sands, the men had started northward toward the Tarim, which was sixty or seventy miles away. If they could reach it, they would find shelter in one of the sparse settlemeats of fishermen along its shores and could eventually make their way back to civilization.

It was now afternoon of the second day of their wanderings. Langley had suffered most, and he staggered a little as they went on beneath the eternally cloudless heavens, across the glaring desolation of the dreary landscape. His heavy Winchester had become an insufferable burden, and he had thrown it away in spite of the remonstrance of Furnham, who still retained his own weapon.

The sun had lowered a little, but burned with gruelling rays, tyrannically torrid, through the bright inferno of stagnant air. There was no wind except for brief and furious puffs that whirled the light sand in the faces of the men and then died as suddenly as they had risen. The ground gave back the heat and glare of the heavens in shimmering, blinding waves of refraction.

Langley and Furnham mounted a low, gradual ridge and paused in sweltering exhaustion on its rocky spine. Before them was a broad, shallow valley, at which they stared in a sort of groggy wonderment, puzzled by the level and artificial-looking depression, perfectly square and perhaps a third of a mile wide, which they descried in its center. The depression was bare and empty with no sign of ruins, but was lined with numerous pits that suggested the ground-plan of a vanished city.

The men blinked, and both were prompted to rub their eyes as they peered through flickering heatwaves, for each had received a momentary impression of flashing light, broken into myriad spires and columns, that seemed to fill the shallow basin and fade like a mirage.

Still mindful of their quarrel, but animated by the same unspoken thought, they started down the long declivity, heading straight toward the depression. If the place were the site of some ancient city they might possibly hope to find a well or water-spring.

They approached the basin's edge and were puzzled more and more by its regularity. Certainly it was not the work of nature, and it might have been quarried yesterday, for seemingly there were no ravages of wind and weather in the sheer walls, and the floor was remarkably smooth, except for the multitude of square pits that ran in straight, intersecting lines like the cellars of destroyed or unbuilt houses. A growing sense of strangeness and mystery troubled the two men, and they were blinded at intervals by the flash of evanescent light that seemed to overflow the basin with phantom towers and pillars.

They paused within a few feet of the edge, incredulous and bewildered. Each began to wonder if his brain had been affected by the sun. Their sensations were such as might mark the incipience of delirium. Amid the blasts of furnace-like heat, a sort of icy coolness appeared to come upon them from the broad basin. Clammy but refreshing, like the chill that might emanate from walls of sunless stone, it revived their fainting senses and quickened their awareness of unexplained mystery.

The coolness became even more noticeable when they reached the very verge of the precipice. Here, peering over, they saw that the sides fell unbroken at all points for a depth of twenty feet or more. In the smooth bottom, the cellar-like pits yawned darkly and unfathomably. The floor about the pits was free of sand, pebbles, or detritus.

"Heavens, what do you make of that?" muttered Furnham to himself rather than to Langley. He stooped over the edge, staring down with feverish and inconclusive speculations. The riddle was beyond his experience — he had met nothing like it in all his researches. His puzzlement, however, was partly submerged in the more pressing problem of how he and Langley were to descend the sheer walls. Thirst — and the hope of finding water in one of the pits — were more important at that moment than the origin and nature of the square basin.

Suddenly, in his stooping position, a kind of giddiness seized him, and the earth seemed to pitch deliriously beneath his feet. He staggered, lost his balance, and fell forward from the verge.

Half fainting, he closed his eyes against the hurtling descent and the crash twenty feet below. Instantly, it seemed, he struck bottom, Amazed and incomprehending, he found that he was lying at full length, prone on his stomach in mid-air, upborne by a hard, flat, invisible substance. His outflung hands encountered an obstruction, cool as ice and smooth as marble, and the chill of it smote through his clothing as he lay gazing down into the gulf. Wrenched from his grasp by the fall, his rifle hung beside him.

He heard the startled cry of Langley and then realized that the latter had seized him by the ankles and was drawing him back to the precipice. He felt the unseen surface slide beneath him, level as a concrete pavement, glib as glass. Then Langley was helping him to his feet. Both, for the nonce, had forgotten their misunderstanding.

"Say, am I bughouse?" cried Langley. "I thought you were a goner when you fell. What have we stumbled on, anyhow?"

"Stumbled is good," said Furnham reflectively as he tried to collect himself. "That basin is floored with something solid, but transparent as air — something unknown to geologists or chemists. God knows what it is or where it came from or who put it there. We've found a mystery that puts Kobar in the shade. I move that we investigate."

He stepped forward, very cautiously, still half-fearful of falling, and stood suspended over the basin.

"If you can do it, I guess I can," said Langley as he followed. With Furnham in the lead, the two began to cross the basin, moving slowly and gingerly along the invisible pavement. The sensation of peering down as if through empty air was indescribably weird.

They had started midway between two rows of the dark pits, which lay fifty feet apart. Somehow, it was like following a street. After they had gone some little distance from the verge, Furnham deviated to the left, with the idea of looking directly down into one of these mysterious pits. Before he could reach a vertical vantage-point, he was arrested by a smooth, solid wall like that of a building.

"I think we've discovered a city," he announced. Groping his way along the air-clear wall, which seemed free of angles or roughness, he came to an open doorway. It was about five feet wide and of indeterminable height. Fingering the wall like a blind man, he found that it was nearly six inches thick. He and Langley entered the door, still walking on a level pavement, and advanced without obstruction, as if in a large empty room.

For an instant, as they went forward, light seemed to flash above them in great arches and arcades, touched with evanescent colors like those in fountain-spray. Then it vanished, and the sun shone down as before from a void and desert-heaven. The coolness emanating from the unknown substance was more pronounced than ever, and the men almost shivered. But they were vastly refreshed, and the torture of their thirst was somewhat mitigated.

Now they could look perpendicularly into the square pit below them in the stone floor of the excavation. They were unable to see its bottom, for it went down into shadow beyond the westering sun-rays. But both could see the bizarre and inexplicable object which appeared to float immobile in air just below the mouth of the pit. They felt a creeping chill that was more insidious, more penetrant than the iciness of the unseen walls.

"Now I'm seeing things," said Langley.

"Guess I'm seeing them, too," added Furnham.

The object was a long, hairless, light-grey body, lying horizontally, as if in some invisible sarcophagus or tomb. Standing erect, it would have been fully seven feet in height. It was vaguely human in its outlines and possessed two legs and two arms; but the head was quite unearthly. The thing seemed to have a double set of high, concave ears, lined with perforations, and in place of nose, mouth, and chin, there was a long, tapering trunk, which lay coiled on the bosom of the monstrosity like a serpent. The eyes — or what appeared to be such — were covered by leathery, lashless, and hideously wrinkled lids.

The thing lay rigid, and its whole aspect was that of a well-perserved corpse or mummy. Half in light and half in shadow, it hung amid the funereal, fathomless pit; and beneath it, at some little distance, as their eyes became accustomed to the gloom, the men seemed to perceive another and similar body.

Neither could voice the mad, eerie thoughts that assailed them. The mystery was too macabre and overwhelming and impossible.

It was Langley who spoke at last.

"Say, do you suppose they are all dead?"

Before Furnham could answer, he and Langley heard a thin, shrill, exiguous sound, like the piping off some unearthly flute whose notes were almost beyond human audition. They could not determine its direction, for it seemed to come from one side and then from another as it continued. Its degree of apparent nearness or distance was also variable. It went on ceaselessly and monotonously, thrilling them with an eeriness as of untrod worlds, a terror as of uncharted dimensions. It seemed to fade away in remote ultramundane gulfs, and then, louder and clearer than before, the piping came from the air beside them.

Inexpressibly startled, the two men stared from side to side in an effort to locate the source of the sound. They could find nothing. The air was clear and still about them, and their view of the rocky slopes that rimmed the basin was blurred only by the dancing haze of heat.

The piping ceased and was followed by a dead, uncanny silence. But Furnham and Langley had the feeling that someone or something was near them — a stealthy presence that lurked and crouched and drew closer till they could have shrieked aloud with the terror of suspense. They seemed to wait amid the unrealities of delirium and mirage, haunted by some elusive, undeclared horror.

Tensely, they peered and listened, but there was no sound or visual ostent. Then Langfey cried out and fell heavily to the unseen floor, borne backward by the onset of a cold and tangible thing, resistless as the launching coils of an anaconda. He lay helpless, unable to move beneath the dead and fluid weight of the unknown incubus which crushed down his limbs and body and almost benumbed him with an icy chill as of etheric space. Then something touched his throat, very lightly at first, and then with a pressure that deepened intolerably to a stabbing pain, as if he had been pierced by an icicle.

A black faintness swept upon him, and the pain seemed to recede as if the nerves that bore it to his brain were spun like lengthening gossamers across gulfs of anesthesia.

Furnham, in a momentary paralysis, heard the cry of his companion and saw Langley fall and struggle feebly, to lie inert with closing eyes and whitening face, Mechanically, without realizing for some moments what had happened, he perceived that Langley's garments were oddly flattened and pressed down beneath an invisible weight. Then, from the hollow of Langley's neck, he saw the spurting of a thin rill of blood, which mounted straight in air for several inches, and vanished in a sort of red mist.

Bizarre, incoherent thoughts arose in Furnham's mind. It was all too incredible, too unreal. His brain must be wandering, it must have given way entirely . . . but something was attacking Langley — an invisible vampire of this invisible city.

He had retained his rifle. Now he stepped forward and stood beside the fallen man. His free hand, groping in the air, encountered a chill, clammy surface, rounded like the back of a stooping body. It numbed his fingertips even as he touched it. Then something seemed to reach out like an arm and hurl him violently backward.

Reeling and staggering, he managed to retain his balance and returned more cautiously. The blood still rose in a vanishing rill from Langley's throat. Estimating the position of the unseen attacker, Furnham raised his rifle and took careful aim, with the muzzle less than a yard away from its hidden mark.

The gun roared with deafening resonance, and its sound died away in slow echoes, as if repeated by a maze of walls. The blood ceased to rise from Langley's neck and fell to a natural trickle. There was no sound, no manifestation of any kind from the thing that had assailed him. Furnham stood in doubt, wondering if his shot had taken effect. Perhaps the thing had been frightened away; perhaps it was still close at hand, and might leap upon him at any moment or return to its prey.

He peered at Langley, who lay white and still. The blood was ceasing to flow from the tiny puncture. He stepped toward him, with the idea of trying to revive him, but was arrested by a strange circumstance. He saw that Langley's face and upper body were blurred by a grey mist that seemed to thicken and assume palpable outlines. It darkened apace; it took on solidity and form, and Furnham beheld the monstrous thing that lay prone between himself and his companion, with part of its fallen bulk still weighing upon Langley. From its inertness and the bullet-wound in its side, whence oozed a viscid purple fluid, he felt sure that the thing was dead.

The monster was alien to all terrestrial biology — a huge, invertebrate body, formed like an elongated starfish, with the points ending in swollen tentacular limbs. It had a round, shapeless head with the curving, needle-tipped bill of some mammoth insect. It must have come from another planet or dimension than ours. It was wholly unlike the mummified creature that floated in the pit below, and Furnham felt that it represented an inferior animal-like type. It was evidently composed of an unknown order of organic matter that became visible to human eyes only in death.

His brain was swamped by the mad enigma of it all. What was this place upon which he and Langley had stumbled? Was it an outpost of worlds beyond human knowledge or observation? What was the material of which these buildings had been wrought? Who were their builders? Whence had they come, and what had been their purpose? Was the city of recent date or was it, perhaps, a sort of ruin whose builders lay dead in its vaults — a ruin haunted only by the vampire monster that had assailed Langley?

Shuddering with repulsion at the dead monster, he started to drag the still-unconscious man from beneath the loathsome mass. He avoided touching the dark, semi-translucent body, which lapsed forward, quivering like a stiff jelly when he had pulled his companion away from it.

Like something very trivial and far away, he remembered the absurd quarrel which Langley had picked with him and remembered his own resentment as part of a doubtful dream, now lost in the extra-human mystery of their surroundings. He bent over his comrade anxiously and saw that some of the natural tan was returning to the pale face and that the eyelids were beggining to flutter. The blood had clotted on the tiny wound. Taking Langley's canteen, he poured the last of its contents between the owner's teeth.

In a few moments, Langley was able to sit up. Furnham helped him to his feet, and the two began to cross their way from the crystal maze.

They found the doorway, and Furnham, still supporting the other, decided to retrace their course along the weird street by which they had started to cross the basin. They had gone but a few paces when they heard a faint, almost inaudible rustling in the air before them, together with a mysterious grating noise. The rustling seemed to spread and multiply on every hand as if an invisible crowd were gathering, but the grating soon ceased.

They went on, slowly and cautiously, with a sense of imminent, uncanny peril. Langley was now strong enough to walk without assistance, and Furnham held his cocked rifle ready for instant use. The vague rustling sounds receded, but still encircled them.

Midway between the underlying rows of pits, they moved on toward the desert precipice, keeping side by side. A dozen paces on the cold, solid pavement, and then they stepped into empty air and landed several feet below with a terrific jar on another hard surface.

It must have been the top of a flight of giant stairs for, losing their balance, they both lurched and fell and rolled downward along a series of similar surfaces and lay stunned at the bottom.

Langley had been rendered unconscious by the fall, but Fornham was vaguely aware of several strange, dreamlike phenomena. He heard a faint, ghostly, sibilant rustling; he felt a light and clammy touch upon his face and smelled an odor of suffocating sweetness, in which he seemed to sink as into an unfathomable sea. The rustling died to a vast and spatial silence; oblivion darkened above him; and he slid swiftly into nothingness.

IT WAS night when Furnham awoke. His first impression was the white dazzle of a full moon shining in his eyes. Then he became aware that the circle of the great orb was oddly distorted and broken, like a moon in some cubist painting. All around and above him were bright, crystalline angles, crossing and intermingling — the outlines of a translucent architecture, dome on dome and wall on wall. As he moved his head, showers of ghostly irises — the lunar yellow and green and purple — fell in his eyes from the broken orb and vanished.

He saw that he was lying on a glasslike floor, which caught the light in moving sparkles. Langley, still unconscious, was beside him. Doubtless they were still in the mysterious oubliette down whose invisible stairs they had fallen. Far off, to one side, through a mélange of the transparent partitions, he could see the vague rocks of the Lob-nor, twisted and refracted in the same manner as the moon.

Why, he wondered, was the city now visible? Was its substance rendered perceptible, in a partial sort of way, by some unknown ray which existed in moonlight but not in the direct beams of the sun? Such an explanation sounded altogether too unscientific, but he could not think of any other at the moment.

Rising on his elbow, he saw the glassy outlines of the giant stairs down which he and Langley had plunged. A pale, diaphanous form, like a phantom of the mummified creature they had seen in the pit, was descending the stairs. It moved forward with fleet strides, longer than those of a man, and stooped above Furnham with its spectral trunk waving inquisitively and poising an inch or two from his face. Two round, phosphorescent eyes, emitting perceptible beams like lanterns, glowed solemnly in its head above the beginning of the proboscis.

The eyes seemed to transfix Furnham with their unearthly gaze. He felt that the light they emitted was flowing in a ceaseless stream into his own eyes — into his very brain. The light seemed to shape itself into images, formless and incomprehensible at first, but growing clearer and more coherent momently. Then, in some indescribable way, the images were associated with articulate words, as if a voice were speaking words that he understood as one might understand the language of dreams.

"We mean you no harm," the voice seemed to say. "But you have stumbled upon our city; and we cannot afford to let you escape. We do not wish to have our presence known to men.

"We have dwelt here for many ages, The Lob-nor desert was a fertile realm when we first established our city. We came to your world as fugitives from a great planet that once formed part of the solar system — a planet, composed entirely of ultra-violet substances, which was destroyed in a terrible cataclysm. Knowing the imminence of the catastrophe, some of us were able to build a huge space-flier, in which we fled to the Earth. From the materials of the flier, and other materials we had brought along for the express purpose, we built our city, whose name, as well as it can be conveyed in human phonetics, is Ciis.

"The things of your world have always been plainly visible to us and, in fact, due to our immense scale of perceptions, we probably see much that is not manifest to you. Also, we have no need of artificial light at any time. We discovered, however, at an early date, that we ourselves and our buildings were invisible to men. Strangely enough, our bodies undergo in death a degeneration of substance which brings them within the infra-violet range and thus within the scope of your visual cognition."

The voice seemed to pause, and Furnham realized that it had spoken only in his thought by a sort of telepathy. In his own mind, he tried to shape a question:

"What do you intend to do with us?"

Again he heard the still, toneless voice:

"We plan to keep you with us permanently. After you fell through the trap-door we had opened, we overpowered you with an anesthetic. During your period of unconsciousness, which lasted many hours, we injected into your bodies a drug which has already affected your vision, rendering visible, to a certain degree, the ultra-violet substances that surround you. Repeated injections, which must be given slowly, will make these substances no less plain and solid to you than the materials of your own world. Also, there are other processes to which we intend to subject you . . . processes that will serve to adjust and acclimate you in all ways to your new surroundings."

Behind Furnham's weird interlocutor, several more fantasmal figures had descended the half-visible steps. One of them was stooping over Langley, who had begun to stir and would recover full consciousness in a few instants. Furnham sought to frame other questions and received an immediate reply.

"The creature that attacked your companion was a domestic animal. We were busy in our laboratories at the time and did not know of your presence till we heard the rifle shots.

"The flashes of light which you saw among our invisible walls on your arrival were due to some queer phenomenon of refraction. At certain angles, the sunlight was broken or intensified by the molecular arrangement of the unseen substance."

At this juncture, Langley sat up, looking about him in a bewildered fashion.

"What the hell is all this, and where the hell are we?" he inquired as he peered from Furnham to the people of the city.

Furnham proceeded to explain, repeating the telepathic information he had just received. By the time he had ceased speaking, Langley himself appeared to become the recipient of some sort of mental reassurance from the phantom-like creature who had been Furnham's interlocutor, for Langley stared at this being with a mixture of enlightenment and wonder in his expression.

Once more there came the still, super-auditory voice, fraught now with imperious command.

"Come with us. Your initiation into our life is to begin immediately. My name is Aispha — if you wish to have a name for me in your thoughts. We ourselves communicating with each other without language, have little need for names, and their use is a rare formality among us. Our generic name, as a people, is the Tiisins."

Furnham and Langley arose with an unquestioning alacrity, for which afterwards they could hardly account, and followed Aispha. It was as if a mesmeric compulsion had been laid upon them. Furnham noted, in an automatic sort of way, as they left the oubliette, that his rifle had vanished. No doubt it had been carefully removed during his period of insensibility.

He and Langley climbed the high steps with some difficulty. Queerly enough, considering their late fall, they found themselves quite free of stiffness and bruises; but at the time, they felt no surprise — only a drugged acquiescence in all the marvels and perplexities of their situation.

They found themselves on the outer pavement, amid the bewildering outlines of the luminous buildings which towered above them with intersections of multiform crystalline curves and angles. Aispha went on without pause, leading them toward the fantastic serpentine arch of an open doorway in one of the tallest of these edifices, whose pale domes and pinnacles were heaped in immaterial splendor athwart the zenith-nearing moon.

Four of the ultra-violet people — the companions of Aispha — brought up the rear. Aispha was apparently unarmed, but the others carried weapons like heavy-bladed and blunt-pointed sickles of glass or crystal Many others of this incredible race, intent on their own enigmatic affairs, were passing to and fro in the open street and through the portals of the unearthly buildings. The city was a place of silent and fantasmal activity.

At the end of the street they were following, before they passed through the arched entrance, Furnham and Langley saw the rock-strewn slope of the Lob-nor, which seemed to have taken on a queer filminess and insubstantiality in the moonlight. It occurred to Furnham, with a sort of weird shock, that his visual perception of earthly objects, as well as of the ultra-violet city, was being affected by the injections of which Aispha told him.

The building they now entered was full of apparatuses made in the form of distorted spheres and irregular disks and cubes, some of which seemed to change their outlines from moment to moment in a confusing manner. Certain of them appeared to concentrate the moonlight like ultra-powerful lenses, turning it to a fiery, blinding brilliance. Neither Furnham nor Langley could imagine the purpose of these devices, and no telepathic explanation was vouchsafed by Aispha or any of his companions.

As they went on into the building, there was a queer sense of some importunate and subtle vibration in the air, which affected the men unpleasantly. They could not assign its source, nor could they be sure whether their own perception of it was purely mental or came through the avenues of one or more of the physical senses. Somehow, it was both disturbing and narcotic, and they sought instinctively to resist its influence.

The lower story of the edifice was seemingly one vast room. The strange apparatuses grew taller about them, rising as if in concentric tiers as they went on. In the huge dome above them, living rays of mysterious light appeared to cross and re-cross at all angles of incidence, weaving a bright, ever-changing web that dazzled the eye.

They emerged in a clear, circular space at the center of the building. Here, ten or twelve of the ultra-violet people were standing about a slim column, perhaps five feet high, that culminated in a shallow basin-like formation. There was a glowing oval-shaped object in the basin, large as the egg of some extinct bird. From this object, numerous spokes of light extended horizontally in all directions, seeming to transfix the heads and bodies of those who stood in a loose ring about the column. Furnham and Langley became aware of a high, thin, humming noise which emanated from the glowing egg and was somehow inseparable from the spokes of light, as if the radiance had become audible.

Aispha paused, facing the men, and a voice spoke in their minds.

"The glowing object is called the Doir. An explanation of its real nature and origin would be beyond your present comprehension. It is allied, however, to that range of substances which you would classify as minerals and is one of a number of similar objects which existed in our former world. It generates a mighty force which is intimately connected with our life-principle, and the rays emanating from it serve us in place of food. If the Doir were lost or destroyed, the consequences would be serious; and our life-term, which normally is many thousand years, would be shortened for want of the nourishing and revivifying rays."

Fascinated, Furnham and Langley stared at the eggshaped orb. The humming seemed to grow louder, and the spokes of light lengthened and increased in number. The men recognized it now as the source of the vibration that had troubled and oppressed them. The effect was insidious, heavy, hypnotic, as if there were a living brain in the object that sought to overcome their volition and subvert their senses and their minds in some unnatural thralldom.

They heard the mental command of Aispha:

"Go forward and join those who partake of the luminous emanations of the Doir. We believe that by so doing you will, in course of time, become purged of your terrestrial grossness, that the very substance of your bodies may eventually be transformed into something not unlike that of our own, and your senses raised to a perceptional power such as we possess."

Half unwillingly, with an eerie consciousness of compulsion, the men started forward.

"I don't like this," said Furnham in a whisper to Langley. "I'm beginning to feel queer enough already." Summoning his utmost will power he stopped short of the emanating rays and put out his hand to arrest Langley.

With dazzled eyes, they stood peering at the Doir. A cold, restless fire, alive with some nameless evil that was not akin to the evil of Earth, pulsated in its heart; and the long, sharp beams, quivering slightly, passed like javelins into the semi-crystalline bodies of the beings who stood immobile around the column.

"Hasten!" came the unvocal admonition of Aispha. "In a few

moments, the force in the Doir, which has a regular rhythm of ebb and flow, will begin to draw back upon itself. The rays will be retracted, and you will have to wait for many minutes before the return of the emanation."

A quick, daring thought had occurred to Furnham. Eyeing the Doir closely, he had been impressed by its seeming fragility. The thing was evidently not attached to the basin in which it reposed; and in all likelihood it would shatter like glass if hurled or even dropped on the floor. He tried to suppress his thought, fearing that it would be read by Aispha or others of the ultra-violet people. At the same time, he sought to phrase, as innocently as possible, a mental question:

"What would happen if the Doir were broken?"

Instantly he received an impression of anger, turmoil and consternation in the mind of Aispha. His question, however, was apparently not answered; and it seemed that Aispha did not want to answer it — that he was concealing something too dangerous and dreadful to be revealed. Furnham felt, too, that Aispha was suspicious, had received an inkling of his own repressed thought.

It occurred to him that he must act quickly if at all. Nerving himself, he leaped forward through the ring of bodies about the Doir. The rays had already begun to shorten slightly, but he had the feeling of one who hurls himself upon an array of lance-points. There was an odd, indescribable sensation, as if he were being pierced by something that was both hot and cold, but neither the warmth nor the chill was beyond endurance. A moment, and he stood beside the column, lifting the glowing egg in his hands and poising it defiantly as he turned to face the ultra-violet people.

The thing was phenomenally light, and it seemed to burn his fingers and to freeze them at the same time. He felt a strange vertigo, an indescribable confusion, but he succeeded in mastering it. The contact of the Doir might be deadlier to the human tissues than that of radium for aught he knew. He would have to take his chances. At any rate, it would not kill him immediately, and if he played his cards with sufficient boldness and skill, he could make possible the escape of Langley — if not his own escape.

The ring of ultra-violet beings stood as if stupefied by his audacity. The retracting spokes of light were slowly drawing back into the egg, but Furnham himself was still impaled by them. His fingers seemed to be growing translucent where they clutched the weird ball.

He met the phosphoric gaze of Aispha and heard the frantic thoughts that were pouring into his mind not only from Aispha, but from all the partakers of the Doir's luminous beams. Dread, unhuman threats, desperate injunctions to return the Doir to its pedestal, were being laid upon him. Rallying all his will, he defied them.

"Let us go free," he said, mentally addressing Aispha. "Give me back my weapon and permit my companion and me to leave your city. We wish you no harm, but we cannot allow you to detain us. Let us go or I will shatter the Doir — will smash it like an egg on the floor."

At the shaping of his destructive thought, a shudder passed among the semi-spectral beings, and he felt the dire fear that his threat had aroused in them. He had been right: the Doir was fragile, and some awful catastrophe, whose nature he could not quite determine, would ensue instantly upon its shattering.

Step by step, glancing frequently about to see that no one approached him by stealth from behind, Furnham returned to Langley's side. The Tiisins drew back from him in evident terror. All the while, he continued to issue his demands and comminations:

"Bring the rifle quickly . . . the weapon you took from me . . . and give it into my companion's hands. Let us go without hindrance or molestation — or I will drop the Doir. When we are outside the city, one of you — one only — shall be permitted to approach us, and I will deliver the Doir to him."

One of the Tiisins left the group to return in less than a minute with Furnham's Winchester. He handed it to Langley, who inspected the weapon carefully and found that it had not been damaged or tampered with in any way. Then, with the ultra-violet creatures following them in manifest perturbation, Furnham and Langley made their way from the building and started along the open street in the general direction (as Langley estimated from the compass he carried) of the Tarim River.

They went on amid the fantastic towering of the crystalline piles, and the people of the city, called as if by some unworded summons, poured from the doorways in an ever-swelling throng and gathered behind them There was no active demonstration of any overt kind, but both the men were increasingly aware of the rage and consternation that had been aroused by Furnham's audacious theft of the Doir — a theft that seemed to be regarded in the light of actual blasphemy.

The hatred of the Tiisins, like a material radiation — dark, sullen, stupefying, stultifying — beat upon them at every step. It seemed to dog their brains and their feet like some viscid medium of nightmare, and their progession toward the Lob-nor slope became painfully slow and tedious.

Before them, from one of the buildings, a tentacled, starfish monster, like the thing that had assailed Langley, emerged and lay crouching in the street as if to dispute their passage. Raising its evil beak, it glared with filmy eyes, but slunk away from their approach as if at the monition of its owners.

Furnham and Langley, passing it with involuntary shivers of repugnance, went on. The air was oppressed with alien, unformulable menace. They felt an abnormal drowsiness creeping upon them. There was an unheard, narcotic music, which sought to overcome their vigilance, to beguile them into slumber.

Furnham's fingers grew numb with the unknown radiations of the Doir, though the sharp beams of light, by accelerative degrees, had withdrawn into its center, leaving only a formless misty glow that filled the weird orb. The thing seemed latent with terrible life and power. The bones of his transparent hand were outlined against it like those of a skeleton.

Looking back, he saw that Aispha followed closely, walking in advance of the other Tiisins. He could not read the thoughts of Aispha as formerly. It was as if a blank, dark wall had been built up. Somehow, he had a premonition of evil — of danger and treachery in some form which he could not understand or imagine.

He and Langley came to the end of the street, where the ultra-violet pavement joined itself to the desert acclivity. As they began their ascent of the slope, both men realized that their visual powers had indeed been affected by the injection treatment of the Tiisins, for the soil seemed to glow beneath them, faintly translucent; and the boulders were like semi-crystalline masses, whose inner structure they could see dimly.

Aispha followed them on the slope, but the other people of Ciis, as had been stipulated by Furnham, paused at the juncture of their streets and buildings with the infra-violet substances of Earth.

After they had gone perhaps fifty yards on the gentle acclivity,

Furnham came to a pause and waited for Aispha, holding out the Doir at arm's length. Somehow, he had a feeling that it was unwise to return the mystic egg, but he would keep his promise, since the people of Ciis had kept their part of the bargain so far.

Aispha took the Doir from Furnham's hands, but his thoughts, whatever they were, remained carefully shrouded. There was a sense of something ominous and sinister about him as he turned and went back down the slope with the fiery egg shining through his body like a great watchful eye. The beams of light were beginning to emanate from its center once more. The two men, looking back ever and anon, resumed their journey. Ciis glimmered below them like the city of a mirage in the moonlit hollow. They saw the ultraviolet people crowding to await Aispha at the end of their streets.

Then, as Aispha neared his fellows, two rays of cold, writhing fire leaped forth from the base of a tower that glittered like glass at the city's verge. Clinging to the ground, the rays ran up the slope with the undulant motion of pythons, following Langley and Furnham at a speed that would soon overtake them.

"They're double-crossing us!" warned Furnham. He caught the Winchester from Langley, dropped to his knees and aimed carefully, drawing a bead on the luminous orb of the Doir through the spectral form of Aispha, who had now reached the city and was about to enter the waiting throng.

"Run!" he called to Langley. "I'll make them pay for their treachery, and perhaps you can get away in the meanwhile."

He pulled the trigger, missing Aispha but dropping at least two of the Tiisins who stood near the Doir. Again, steadily, he drew bead, while the rays from the tower serpentined onward, pale, chill and deadly-looking, till they were almost at his feet. Even as he aimed, Aispha took refuge in the foremost ranks of the crowd, through whose filmy bodies the Doir still glowed.

This time the high-powered bullet found its mark, though it must have passed through more than one of the ultra-violet beings before reaching Aispha and the mystic orb.

Furnham had hardly known what the result would be, but he felt sure that some sort of catastrophe would ensue the destruction of the Doir. What really happened was incalculable and almost beyond description. Before the Doir could fall from the hands of its stricken bearer, it seemed to expand in a rushing wheel of intense light, revolving as it grew and blotting out the forms of the ultra-violet people in the foreground. With awful velocity, the wheel struck the nearer buildings, which appeared to soar and vanish like towers of fading mirage. There was no audible explosion — no sound of any kind — only that silent, ever-spinning, ever-widening disk of light that threatened to involve by swift degrees the whole extent of Ciis.

Gazing spellbound, Furnham had almost forgotten the serpentine rays. Too late, he saw that one of them was upon him. He leaped back, but the thing caught him, coiling about his limbs and body like an anaconda. There was a sensation of icy cold, of horrible constriction, and then, helpless, he found that the strange beam of force was dragging him back down the slope toward Ciis, while its fellow went on in pursuit of the fleeing Langley.

In the meanwhile, the spreading disk of fire had reached the tower from which the ray emanated. Suddenly, Furnham was free — the serpentine beams had both vanished. He stood rooted to the spot in speechless awe, and Langley, returning down the hill, also paused, watching the mighty circle of light that seemed to fill the entire basin at their feet with a soundless vortex of destruction.

"My God!" cried Furnham after a brief interval. "Look what's happening to the slope."

As if the force of the uncanny explosion were now extending beyond Ciis, boulders and masses of earth began to rise in air before the white, glowing maelstron, and they sailed in slow, silent levitation toward the men.

Furnham and Langley started to run, stumbling up the slope, and were overtaken by something that lifted them softly, buoyantly, irresistibly, with a strange feeling of utter weightlessness, and bore them like windwafted leaves or feathers through the air. They saw the bouldered crest of the acclivity flowing far beneath them, and then they were floating, floating, ever higher in the moonlight, above leagues of dim desert. A faintness came upon them both — a vague nausea — an illimitable vertigo — and slowly, somewhere in that incredible flight, they lapsed into unconsciousness.

THE MOON had fallen low, and its rays were almost horizontal in Furnham's eyes when he awoke. An utter confusion possessed him at first, and his circumstances were more than bewildering. He was lying on a sandy slope, among scattered shrubs, meager and stunted; and Langley was reclining not far away. Raising himself a little, he saw the white and reed-fringed surface of a river — which could be no other than the Tarim — at the slope's bottom. Half incredulous, he realized that the force of the weird explosion had carried Langley and himself many miles and had deposited them, apparently unhurt, beside the goal of their desert wandering!

Furnham rose to his feet, feeling a queer lightness and unsteadiness. He took a tentative step — and landed four or five feet away. It was as if he had lost half his normal weight. Moving with great care, he went over to Langley, who had now started to sit up. He was reassured to find that his eyesight was becoming normal again, for he perceived merely a faint glowing in the objects about him. The sand and boulders were comfortably solid, and his own hands were no longer translucent.

"Gosh!" he said to Langley. "That was some explosion. The force that was liberated by the shattering of the Doir must have done something to the gravity of all surrounding objects. I guess the city of Ciis and its people must have gone back into outer space, and even the infra-violet substances about the city must have been more or less degravitated. But I guess the effect is wearing off as far as you and I are concerned — otherwise we'd be traveling still."

Langley got up and tried to walk, with the same disconcerting result that had characterized Furnham's attempt. He mastered his limbs and his equilibrium after a few experiments.

"I still feel like a sort of dirigible," he commented. "Say, I think we'd better leave this out of our report to the museum. A city, a people, all invisible, in the heart of the Lob-nor — that would be too much for scientific credibility."

"I agree with you," said Furnham. "The whole business would be too fantastic outside of a super-scientific story. In fact," he added a little maliciously, "it's even more incredible than the existence of the ruins of Kobar."

MOTHER OF TOADS

"WHY MUST YOU always hurry away, my little one?"

The voice of Mère Antoinette, the witch, was an amorous croaking. She ogled Pierre, the apothecary's young apprentice, with eyes full-orbed and unblinking as those of a toad. The folds beneath her chin swelled like the throat of some great batrachian. Her huge breasts, pale as frog-bellies, bulged from her torn gown as she leaned toward him.

He gave no answer, and she came closer, till he saw in the hollow of those breasts a moisture glistening like the dew of marshes . . . like the slime of some amphibian . . . a moisture that seemed always to linger there.

Her voice, raucously coaxing, persisted. "Stay awhile tonight, my pretty orphan. No one will miss you in the village. And your master will not mind." She pressed against him with shuddering folds of fat. With her short, flat fingers, which gave almost the appearance of being webbed, she seized his hand and drew it to her bosom.

Pierre wrenched the hand away and drew back discreetly. Repelled, rather than abashed, he averted his eyes. The witch was more than twice his age, and her charms were too uncouth and unsavory to tempt him for an instant. Also, her repute was such as to have nullified the attractions of a younger and fairer sorceress. Her witchcraft had made her feared among the peasantry of that remote province, where belief in spells and philters was still common. The people of Averoigne called her *La Mere des Crapauds*, Mother of Toads, a name given for more than one reason. Toads swarmed innumerably about her hut; they were said to be her familiars, and dark tales were told concerning their relationship to the sorceress, and the duties they performed at her bidding. Such tales were all the more readily believed because of those batrachian features that had always been remarked in her aspect.

The youth disliked her, even as he disliked the sluggish, abnormally large toads on which he had sometimes trodden in the dusk, upon the path between her hut and the village of Les Hiboux. He could hear some of these creatures croaking now, and it seemed, weirdly, that they uttered half-articulate echoes of the witch's words.

It would be dark soon, he reflected. The path along the marshes was not pleasant by night, and he felt doubly anxious to depart. Still without replying to Mère Antionette's invitation, he reached for the black triangular vial she had set before him on her greasy table. The vial contained a philter of curious potency which his master, Alain le Dindon, had sent him to procure. Le Dindon, the village apothecary, was wont to deal surreptitiously in certain dubious medicaments supplied by the witch, and Pierre had often gone on such errands to her osier-hidden hut.

The old apothecary, whose humor was rough and ribald, had sometimes rallied Pierre concerning Mère Antoinette's preference for him. "Some night, my lad, you will remain with her," he had said. "Be careful, or the big toad will crush you." Remembering this gibe, the boy flushed angrily as he turned to go.

"Stay," insisted Mère Antoinette. "The fog is cold on the marshes, and it thickens apace. I knew that you were coming, and I have mulled for you a goodly measure of the red wine of Ximes."

She removed the lid from an earthen pitcher and poured its steaming contents into a large cup. The purplish-red wine creamed delectably, and an odor of hot, delicious spices filled the hut, overpowering the less agreeable odors from the simmering cauldron, the half-dried newts, vipers, bat-wings, and evil, nauseous herbs hanging on the walls, and the reek of the black candles of pitch and corpse-tallow that burned always, by noon or night, in that murky interior.

"I'll drink it," said Pierre, a little grudgingly. "That is, if it contains nothing of your own concoction."

"'Tis naught but sound wine, four seasons old, with spices of Arabia," the sorceress croaked ingratiatingly. "'Twill warm your stomach . . . and . . ." She added something inaudible as Pierre accepted the cup.

Before drinking, he inhaled the fumes of the beverage with some caution but was reassured by its pleasant smell. Surely it was innocent of any drug, any philter brewed by the witch for, to his knowledge, her preparations were all evil-smelling.

Still, as if warned by some premonition, he hesitated. Then he remembered that the sunset air was indeed chill; that mists had gathered furtively behind him as he came to Mère Antoinette's dwelling. The wine would fortify him for the dismal return walk to Les Hiboux. He quaffed it quickly and set down the cup.

"Truly, it is good wine," he declared. "But I must go now."

Even as he spoke, he felt in his stomach and veins the spreading warmth of the alcohol, of the spices . . . of something more ardent than these. It seemed that his voice was unreal and strange, falling as if from a height above him. The warmth grew, mounting within him like a golden flame fed by magic oils. His blood, a seething torrent, poured tumultuously and more tumultuously through his members.

There was a deep, soft thundering in his ears, a rosy dazzlement in his eyes. Somehow, the hut appeared to expand, to change luminously about him. He hardly recognized its squalid furnishings, its litter of baleful oddments, on which a torrid splendor was shed by the black candles, tipped with ruddy fire, that towered and swelled gigantically into the soft gloom His blood burned as with the throbbing flame of the candles.

It came to him, for an instant, that all this was a questionable enchantment, a glamor wrought by the witch's wine. Fear was upon him, and he wished to flee. Then, close beside him, he saw Mère Antoinette.

Briefly, he marvelled at the change that had befallen her. Then fear and wonder were alike forgotten, together with his old repulsion. He knew why the magic warmth mounted ever higher and hotter within him, why his flesh glowed like the ruddy tapers.

The soiled skirt she had worn lay at her feet, and she stood naked as Lilith, the first witch. The lumpish limbs and body had grown voluptuous; the pale, thick-lipped mouth enticed him with a promise of ampler kisses than other mouths could yield. The pits of her short, round arms, the concave of her ponderously drooping breasts, the heavy creases and swollen rondures of flanks and thighs, all were fraught with luxurious allurement.

"Do you like me now, my little one?" she questioned.

This time, he did not draw away but met her with hot, questing hands when she pressed heavily against him. Her limbs were cool and moist; her breasts yielded like the turf-mounds above a bog. Her body was white and wholly hairless, but here and there he found curious roughnesses . . . like those on the skin of a toad . . . that somehow sharpened his desire instead of repelling it.

She was so huge that his fingers barely joined behind her, His two hands, together, were equal only to the cupping of a single breast. But the wine had filled his blood with a philterous ardor.

She led him to her couch beside the hearth where a great cauldron boiled mysteriously, sending up its fumes in strange-twining coils that suggested vague and obscene figures. The couch was rude and bare. But the flesh of the sorceress was like deep, luxurious cushions...

PIERRE AWOKE in the ashy dawn, when the tall, black tapers had dwindled down and had melted limply in their sockets. Sick and confused, he sought vainly to remember where he was or what he had done. Then, turning a little, he saw beside him on the couch a thing that was like some impossible monster of ill dreams; a toadlike form, large as a fat woman. Its limbs were somehow like a woman's arms and legs. Its pale, warty body pressed and bulged against him, and he felt the rounded softness of something that resembled a breast.

Nausea rose within him as memory of that delirious night returned. Most foully he had been beguiled by the witch and had succumbed to her evil enchantments.

It seemed that an incubus smothered him, weighing upon all his limbs and body. He shut his eyes that he might no longer behold the loathsome thing that was Mère Antoinette in her true semblance. Slowly, with prodigious effort, he drew himself away from the crushing nightmare shape. It did not stir or appear to waken; and he slid quickly from the couch.

Again, compelled by a noisome fascination, he peered at the thing on the couch — and saw only the gross form of Mère Antoinette. Perhaps his impression of a great toad beside him had been but an illusion, a half dream that lingered after slumber. He lost something of his nightmarish horror, but his gorge still rose in a sick disgust, remembering the lewdness to which he had yielded.

Fearing that the witch might awaken at any moment and seek to detain him, he stole noiselessly from the hut. It was broad daylight, but a cold, hueless mist lay everywhere, shrouding the reedy marshes, and hanging like a ghostly curtain on the path he must follow to Les Hiboux. Moving and seething always, the mist seemed to reach toward him with intercepting fingers as he started homeward. He shivered at its touch; he bowed his head and drew his cloak closer around him.

Thicker and thicker the mist swirled, coiling, writhing endlessly, as if to bar Pierre's progress. He could discern the twisting, narrow path for only a few paces in advance. It was hard to find the familiar landmarks, hard to recognize the osiers and willows that loomed suddenly before him like gray phantoms and faded again into the white nothingness as he went onward. Never had he seen such fog: it was like the blinding, stifling fumes of a thousand witch-stirred cauldrons.

Though he was not altogether sure of his surroundings, Pierre thought that he had covered half the distance to the village. Then, all at once, he began to meet the toads. They were hidden by the mist till he came close upon them. Misshapen, unnaturally big and bloated, they squatted in his way on the little footpath or hopped sluggishly before him from the pallid gloom on either hand.

Several struck against his feet with a horrible and heavy flopping. He stepped unaware upon one of them and slipped in the squashy noisomeness it had made, barely saving himself from a headlong fall on the bog's rim. Black, miry water gloomed close beside him as he staggered there.

Turning to regain his path, he crushed others of the toads to an abhorrent pulp under his feet. The marshy soil was alive with them. They flopped against him from the mist, striking his legs, his bosom, his very face with their clammy bodies. They rose up by scores like a devil-driven legion. It seemed that there was a malignance, an evil purpose in their movements, in the buffeting of their violent impact. He could make no progress on the swarming path, but lurched to and fro, slipping blindly and shielding his face with lifted hands. He felt an eery consternation, an eldrich horror. It was as if the nightmare of his awakening in the witch's hut had somehow returned upon him.

The toads came always from the direction of Les Hiboux, as if to drive him back toward Mère Antoinette's dwelling. They bounded against him like a monstrous hail, like missiles flung by unseen demons. The ground was covered by them, the air was filled with their hurtling bodies. Once, he nearly went down beneath them.

Their number seemed to increase; they pelted him in a noxious storm. He gave way before them, his courage broke, and he started to run at random, without knowing that he had left the safe path. Losing all thought of direction in his frantic desire to escape from those impossible myriads, he plunged on amid the dim reeds and sedges, over ground that quivered gelatinously beneath him. Always at his heels, he heard the soft, heavy flopping of the toads; and sometimes they rose up like a sudden wall to bar his way and turn him aside. More than once, they drove him back from the verge of hidden quagmires into which he would otherwise have fallen. It was as if they were herding him deliberately and concertedly to a destined goal.

Now, like the lifting of a dense curtain, the mist rolled away, and Pierre saw before him in a golden dazzle of morning sunshine the green, thick-growing osiers that surrounded Mère Antoinette's hut. The toads had all disappeared, though he could have sworn that hundreds of them were hopping close about him an instant previously. With a feeling of helpless fright and panic, he knew that he was still within the witch's toils; that the toads were indeed her familiars, as so many people believed them to be. They had prevented his escape and had brought him back to the foul creature . . . whether woman, batrachian, or both . . . who was known as The Mother of Toads.

Pierre's sensations were those of one who sinks momentarily deeper into some black and bottomless quicksand. He saw the witch emerge from the hut and come toward him. Her thick fingers, with pale folds of skin between them like the beginnings of a web, were stretched and flattened on the steaming cup that she carried. A sudden gust of wind arose as if from nowhere, lifting the scanty skirts of Mère Antoinette about her fat thighs and bearing to Pierre's nostrils the hot, familiar spices of the drugged wine.

"Why did you leave so hastily, my little one?" There was an amorous wheedling in the very tone of the witch's question. "I should not have let you go without another cup of the good red wine, mulled and spiced for the warming of your stomach . . . See, I have prepared it for you . . . knowing that you would return."

She came very close to him as she spoke, leering and sidling, and held the cup toward his lips. Pierre grew dizzy with the strange fumes and turned his head away. It seemed that a paralyzing spell had seized his muscles, for the simple movement required an immense effort.

His mind, however, was still clear, and the sick revulsion of that nightmare dawn returned upon him. He saw again the great toad that had lain at his side when he awakened.

"I will not drink your wine," he said firmly. "You are a foul witch, and I loathe you. Let me go."

"Why do you loathe me?" croaked Mère Antoinette. "You loved me yesternight. I can give you all that other women give . . . and more."

"You are not a woman," said Pierre. "You are a big toad. I saw you in your true shape this morning. I'd rather drown in the marsh-waters than sleep with you again."

An indescribable change came upon the sorceress before Pierre had finished speaking. The leer slid from her thick and pallid features, leaving them blankly inhuman for an instant. Then her eyes bulged and goggled horribly, and her whole body appeared to swell as if inflated with venom.

"Go, then!" she spat with a guttural virulence. "But you will soon wish that you had stayed . . ."

The queer paralysis had lifted from Pierre's muscles. It was as if the injunction of the angry witch had served to revoke an insidious, half-woven spell. With no parting glance or word, Pierre turned from her and fled with long, hasty steps, almost running, on the path to Les Hiboux.

He had gone little more than a hundred paces when the fog began to return. It coiled shoreward in vast volumes from the marshes, it poured like smoke from the very ground at his feet. Almost instantly, the sun dimmed to a wan silver disk and disappeared. The blue heavens were lost in the pale and seething voidness overhead. The path before Pierre was blotted out till he seemed to walk on the sheer rim of a white abyss that moved with him as he went.

Like the clammy arms of specters, with death-chill fingers that clutched and caressed, the weird mists drew closer still about Pierre. They thickened in his nostrils and throat, they dripped in a heavy dew from his garments. They choked him with the fœtor of rank waters and putrescent ooze . . . and a stench as of liquefying corpses that had risen somewhere to the surface amid the fen.

Then, from the blank whiteness, the toads assailed Pierre in a surging, solid wave that towered above his head and swept him from the dim path with the force of falling seas as it descended. He went down, splashing and floundering, into water that swarmed with the numberless batrachians. Thick slime was in his mouth and nose as he struggled to regain his footing. The water, however, was only knee-deep, and the bottom, though slippery and oozy, supported him with little yielding when he stood erect.

He discerned indistinctly through the mist the nearby margin from which he had fallen. But his steps were weirdly and horribly hampered by the toad-seething waters when he strove to reach it. Inch by inch, with a hopeless panic deepening upon him, he fought toward the solid shore. The toads leaped and tumbled about him with a dizzying eddylike motion. They swirled like a viscid undertow around his feet and shins. They swept and swelled in great loathsome undulations against his retarded knees.

However, he made slow and painful progress till his outstretched fingers could almost grasp the wiry sedges that trailed from the low bank. Then, from that mist-bound shore, there fell and broke upon him a second deluge of those demoniac toads, and Pierre was borne helplessly backward into the filthy waters.

Held down by the piling and crawling masses, and drowning in nauseous darkness at the thick-oozed bottom, he clawed feebly at his assailants. For a moment, ere oblivion came, his fingers found among them the outlines of a monstrous form that was somehow toadlike... but large and heavy as a fat woman. At the last, it seemed to him that two enormous breasts were crushed closely down upon his face.

Printed in Great Britain
by Amazon